PUFFIN BOOKS

THERE'S A TROLL AT THE BOTTOM OF MY GARDEN

When Selima, Darren and Patrick find a troll hiding in the garden shed, they're really excited. Especially when they discover that this troll doesn't eat people, it eats ice-cream! They decide to look after it during the holidays, that is, until their parents find out. Their parents are not so sure. They think the troll might be the cause of all the litter in the street. But the children and the troll have a plan, and it's a plan that will keep Sebastopol Gardens clean, and green, for ever.

Ann Jungman was a teacher for many years. She has lived in England and in Australia and has written several books including *Vlad the Drac* and *Lucy and the Wolf*. This is her second book for Puffin.

By the same author

LEILA'S MAGICAL MONSTER PARTY

Ann Jungman

There's a Troll at the Bottom of my Garden

Illustrated by Doffy Weir

PUFFIN BOOKS

*To Hannah,
Zoe and Sophie,
with love*

PUFFIN BOOKS

Published by the Penguin Group
Penguin Books Ltd, 27 Wrights Lane, London W8 5TZ, England
Penguin Books USA Inc., 375 Hudson Street, New York, New York 10014, USA
Penguin Books Australia Ltd, Ringwood, Victoria, Australia
Penguin Books Canada Ltd, 10 Alcorn Avenue, Toronto, Ontario, Canada M4V 3B2
Penguin Books (NZ) Ltd, 182–190 Wairau Road, Auckland 10, New Zealand

Penguin Books Ltd, Registered Offices: Harmondsworth, Middlesex, England

First published by Viking 1991
Published in Puffin Books 1993
10 9 8 7 6 5 4 3 2

Text copyright © Ann Jungman, 1991
Illustrations copyright © Doffy Weir, 1991
All rights reserved

The moral right of the author has been asserted

Filmset in Times (Linotron 202)

Printed in England by Clays Ltd, St Ives plc

Contents

Chapter 1
The Garden

The children of Sebastopol
Avenue were fed up. They
were very, very fed up. It was
the summer holidays but all

their parents had told them
not to play in the street.

"Don't be silly," said
Mrs Gorman to Patrick.

"Just look at all that broken glass lying around."

"Certainly not!" said Mrs Singh to Selima. "It's not a

place for children to play. Look at all the disgusting things that are written up on the walls. No, you cannot play out there."

"Just you forget it, son," said Mr Brook to Darren. "That is not a clean place out there. Just look at the rubbish people throw around. Old bottles and cans, paper from fish and chips, boxes from hamburgers. All that stuff just piles up and rots. No, son, either you stay in or you play in the garden. But I won't have you playing out in that street."

So the children decided to

play cricket or football or
rounders. The three children
played until their ball went
over the wall into the garden
next door and no one dared go
and fetch it.

"What shall we do now?"
asked Selima.

"I don't know," moaned
Darren.

"We could watch TV," said
Patrick.

The children fell silent.
Then, suddenly, Patrick said:

"Listen. Can you hear that?"

"What?"

"A low singing sound. I think it's coming from that shed at the bottom of the garden."

They all listened hard. What

they heard was someone
singing quietly:

"I'm a troll, fol-de-rol,
I'm a troll, fol-de-rol."

"Funny," said Selima.
"Whoever is in there is singing
the troll song from 'The Three
Billy-Goats Gruff'."

"It must be one of the other
kids playing a trick," said
Darren. "Let's creep up and
give whoever it is a shock."

"Great!" said Selima.

"Right," said Patrick.

So the three children crept
towards the shed, trying not to
giggle. When they got to it

Darren pulled the door open.
The three children peered into
the darkness.

"We must have been hearing
things," said Darren. "There's
no one here."

"Yes, there is," shouted Selima. "I can see someone sitting in the corner."

As their eyes got used to the dark the children saw a large figure sitting at the far end of the shed.

"Who are you?" asked Darren, trying not to sound scared, but the figure continued to sing:

"I'm a troll, fol-de-rol,
I'm a troll, fol-de-rol,
I'm a troll, fol-de-rol,
And I'll eat you for my
    supper."

The small, hesitant voice didn't fit the fierce words at all.

"Come out with your hands on your head," said Selima, bravely.

The three children hardly breathed as the figure began to move.

Chapter 2
The Troll

A moment or two later a large
figure came out of the shed. To
the children's surprise it really
was a troll. Tears were running

down the troll's face. The
children felt sorry for him.

"I don't think he's going to
eat us for his supper," said
Patrick. "Are you?"

"No," wept the troll. "I
don't like eating people any
more. And I don't like eating
goats any more. They're tough
and hard to eat."

"What do you like eating then?" asked Darren.

"Ice-cream," whispered the troll. "And I'm very hungry."

"We could get you some ice-cream," Selima told him. "Come on, everyone. Let's see how much money we've got."

Selima went home to empty her money box.

Patrick went off to see how much money he could persuade his mum to give him.

Darren emptied his pockets and found a few coins.

When Patrick and Selima came back they found they had enough money to buy the troll one big block of ice-cream.

"We won't be long," they told the troll. "You stay here and we'll go over to the shop and buy the ice-cream. We'll be straight back."

They soon returned with the
ice-cream, unwrapped it, and
the troll began to eat greedily.
The children watched, licking
their lips. The troll licked the
cardboard package, not missing

one delicious drop. Then he
sighed happily and smiled.

"Thank you," he said.
"Thank you very much."

"What are you doing here?"
asked Patrick.

"My rickedy, rackedy bridge
was pulled down," the troll

said sadly. "And a big road
was built. There were lots and
lots of cars. It wasn't a nice
place for a troll any more. So I
left and walked and walked. In
the end I saw this shed and
came in. Now I don't know
what to do or where to go."

The troll started to cry again.

"Don't cry," said Patrick. "You can stay in this shed. We won't tell anybody. And we'll bring you ice-cream every day."

"You are nice," said the troll. "I am very grateful. This is the first nice thing that has happened to me for ages."

So the children saved their pocket money and spent it all on ice-cream for the troll. In return he told them stories of the old days, when he had been very wicked.

"I used to sit under my

rickedy, rackedy bridge," he
told them, "and I would scare
everyone who wanted to cross
over. It was good fun."

The children had such a
good time they forgot to be cross
about not being allowed out to
play in the street. Instead, they
fed the troll and listened to his
stories. Then, one Saturday,

Mrs Singh looked out of her
kitchen window. She saw
Selima walking down the
garden path towards the
shed in Darren's garden. A
moment later she saw Patrick

and Darren following her. They were carrying two tubs of ice-cream, one strawberry and one chocolate chip.

"Something very odd is going on," she thought. "I'll go and have a word with Darren's parents."

So Mrs Singh went next door and told Mr and Mrs Brook what she had seen.

"The boy is going a bit crazy, wanting to eat ice-cream all day long in the garden shed," declared Darren's father. "We'd better go and have a word with the Gormans about this. Maybe they know

something we don't."

They trooped over to number 23.

"I don't understand it at all," said Patrick's mum. "Pat has been no trouble lately. He's stopped moaning about not being allowed to play out. All he does is ask for money."

"Well, I think the answer lies in the garden shed," said Mr Brook. "I suggest we go and give our children a bit of a surprise."

A few moments later all the parents were marching down the garden path towards the garden shed.

Mr Brook pulled the door open – and there sat the troll, eating ice-cream and chatting to the children.

Chapter 3
Found Out

The parents stared at the troll and said nothing. After a while, Mr Brook said:

"And who are you?"

The troll looked at him and tried not to cry.

"I'm a troll, fol-de-rol,
I'm a troll, fol-de-rol,
I'm a troll, fol-de-rol,
And I'll eat you for my
supper."

"Get away!" said Mrs Gorman. "After all that ice-cream you've just eaten?"

"A troll can always eat more," said the troll, trying to look brave.

"Then why didn't you eat the children?" asked Mrs Singh.

"Because trolls don't eat

children," replied the troll,
standing up and showing his
muscles. "They only eat big
people."

"It's not true," said Darren.
"He's only trying to impress
you. He's a very nice troll.
He's been living in this shed for
ages and he hasn't done any
harm."

"Living in my shed, eh?" said Mr Brook. "And how do you know he hasn't done any harm? Maybe he's been here for years and it's him that litters up the street at night."

"Yes, and stamps on all the flowers," agreed Mrs Gorman.

"And writes rude things all over the walls," said Mrs Singh.

"I didn't, I didn't!" cried the troll. "I'm much too scared to go out at night. I haven't done anything. Really and truly."

46

"And I bet he's the one who empties the dustbins out all over the pavement," continued Mr Brook.

"No, I don't, really," wept the troll.

"And you throw newspaper and all sorts into my front garden," added Mrs Singh.

"I don't, I don't," cried the troll miserably.

"And break glass in the road, where it can cut people," said Mrs Gorman.

"No, no, all I've done is sing and eat ice-cream."

"I think we should hand him over to the police and be done

with it," said Mrs Gorman.

"I think you're all being
horrible," Darren burst out. "I
mean, we don't *know* if he has
done anything. I think you
should give him a chance to

prove that he hasn't done it."

"I have to say that I think
Darren does have a point,"
said his father. "I mean, if we
did hand him over to the police
and it turned out that he had

nothing to do with it, we'd feel
pretty bad."

"Mum," said Selima, "be
fair. Please give the troll a
chance."

"Yes!" cried Patrick. "The troll is our friend and if you hand him over, I'll never talk to any of you again."

"Think of a way of testing him," said Darren. "And if he *is* causing all the mess, we'll agree with whatever you decide to do."

"Now listen," said Mr Brook. "I've got a plan. We'll lock the troll in our cellar tonight. And I'll keep watch and make sure he doesn't go out."

"Yes," cried Selima. "And then if there is still rubbish all over the street, we'll know for sure the troll didn't do it."

"Eh, can I have a say, please?" said the troll, looking upset.

Everyone stopped talking and looked at him.

"I would be very frightened if you locked me in a cellar on my own. So could I have a night-light, please?"

"I can't see why not," said Mrs Brook.

"I agree then," said the troll. "If you really think it's the only way."

So that night, after supper, the troll was taken down to the Brooks' cellar. Selima took

some cushions for him. Darren
had a huge block of ice-cream
and a spoon. Patrick took him
some games and some comics
and his Walkman. The troll
looked round the cellar and
said:

"It's nice down here. Much
better than that dirty old
shed."
That night they all went to

bed. Except, that is, for Mr Brook. He sat all night in a chair outside the locked cellar door.

Chapter 4
The Pa-troll!

The next morning the children rushed to their bedroom windows.

Selima looked out. The flowers in the gardens had been crushed.

"Hurray, it wasn't our troll!"
Darren looked out and saw
that a new lot of rubbish had
been dumped on the grass.

"Yippee! It wasn't our troll."
Patrick looked out and saw
newspaper and cans all over
the street.

"Fantastic, it can't have
been our troll!"
That morning the three

families gathered in the Singhs' house. They drank tea and ate biscuits. Except, that is, for the troll, who had a huge block of toffee and nut ice-cream.

"I'm very sorry about last night," said Mr Brook. "It obviously wasn't you messing up the street."

"Don't worry about it," said the troll. "No hard feelings. But I have an idea. I am going to make an offer to the people who live in this street that they can't refuse."

"What's that?"

"That, in return for as much ice-cream as I can eat, I will

patrol this area for you at night
and protect the street."

"How would you do that?"
they all asked.

"Well," said the troll. "Take your choice. I could offer you:

a foot patrol

or an air patrol

or an armoured patrol

or a bicycle patrol."

"Hmm," said Mrs Singh. "It might work."

"Worth a try," said Mr Gorman. "Cheap at the price."

"Why not," agreed the Brooks.

"I think we should start with a foot patrol and see how it goes," said Mrs Gorman.

So, every night, while the people who lived in the road slept, the troll would walk round and make sure no one left dirt and litter in the street. All along the street were notices:

From the first night of the
patrol there were no more
broken bottles, no more
dumped rubbish, no more
gardens trampled, no more

newspapers and old cans. It
was the cleanest and tidiest
street in the neighbourhood.

Soon the children were
allowed out to play again.

They rode their bikes up and down, they played tennis and cricket in their little playground. They played hide-and-seek and all sorts of other games. The children would have liked the troll to come out and play with them, but each day on the door of his shed they found a notice:

Night worker.
Troll asleep.
Do _not_ wake up.

So the children would tiptoe away, leaving sweets and comics and books for their friend.

Chapter 5
The Litter
Brigade

Within a few weeks of the foot
patrol starting, Sebastopol
Avenue became the cleanest
and tidiest street you could

imagine. However, no one was
very happy.

"My Gran hasn't been over
to see us for weeks,"
complained Darren.

"My friends from school

always make an excuse when I
ask them home for tea," added
Selima.

"I think people are
frightened of the troll,"
declared Patrick. "My mate

says he was dared five pounds to walk down this street at night but he was too scared."

"That's daft," said Selima. "Our troll wouldn't hurt a fly."

"*You* know that and *I* know that," Patrick replied. "But strangers don't, and the troll does look pretty fierce."

"Yes," agreed Darren. "And all the notices he put up are very off-putting."

"Sometimes I think I liked it better when the street was filthy but we had lots of visitors," added Selima.

"I know," agreed Patrick. "Even the ice-cream van driver

is too scared to come to this street."

"Yes," said Darren. "And the window cleaner keeps making excuses for not coming to clean the windows."

"And," continued Patrick,
"when old Mrs Fennel got sick
last week, the district nurse did
not want to come and visit
her."

"When our loo got blocked

up," Patrick told them, "we
had a terrible job finding a
plumber; we had to get
someone in from miles away
who hadn't heard of the patrol.
And he said he wouldn't have
come if he'd known what was

going on in our street."

"It wasn't such a good idea
after all," sighed Selima.

"My dad's going to hold a
meeting to which he will invite
all the people living in the
street," Patrick told them. "He

thinks it's gone far enough – I
mean – we didn't realize that
having a patrol would lead to
the street being cut off."

The meeting was held the

following Thursday evening
and all the families who lived
in the street crammed into the
Gormans' sitting-room. At the
front, with Mr Gorman, Mrs

Singh and Mr Brook, sat the troll.

"Fellow residents of Sebastopol Avenue," began Mr Gorman. "I decided to hold this meeting because I know a lot of you are worried about the new situation in our street. Now I'm sure I speak for everyone when I say how delighted we are that the street is so much cleaner; however, it is causing some concern that our patrol system is driving away any possible visitors."

"That's right, my grandchildren are too scared to visit," someone shouted.

"Yeah, and my friends won't come round for our weekly game of bingo," cried another person.

"We like the street being cleaner," said someone else, "but the price is too high."

Lots of heads nodded.

Tears ran down the troll's
face. "I worked so hard," he
whispered. "I was only trying
to help."

"No one is blaming you,"
explained Darren, holding the
troll's paw.

"They are, they are," wept
the troll. "You'll send me away

and there won't be any friends
to play with, or any ice-cream,
or a job for me to do that makes
me feel a part of the street."

And he buried his head in his paws and wept loudly.

"Don't worry, troll," said Selima and comforted him. "We won't send you away."

"You will, you will," sobbed the troll. "I'll be all alone again – lonely and unwanted."

The residents of Sebastopol Avenue looked at the troll and wondered what to do next.

"I've got an idea," said Darren. "An absolutely brilliant idea."

"What's that?" asked his father suspiciously.

"Well, we want the street to be clean and safe but we don't

want everyone scared away by
the patrol, so why don't we get
the troll to organize the
clearing of the rubbish every
day rather than patrolling at
night?"

"The boy is a genius,"

said Mr Brook proudly.

"What a good idea," said everyone. "That way we'd get the best of both worlds."

"Troll," said Mrs Gorman. "Would you do the street the honour of becoming the local

Litter-Organizer-in-Chief?"

"Yes, all right," whispered
the troll and managed a little
smile.

"I've got an even better
idea," said Mrs Singh.
"Instead of just throwing the
rubbish away, why don't we
think of ways of reusing
things? Let's separate the
bottles from the other rubbish
and take them round to the
bottle bank once a week."

"Wonderful idea," cried
everyone.

"Yes. And let's keep all the
paper and take it round to a
recycling centre."

"And all the old fruit and vegetables that will rot can go on my compost heap to make natural manure."

"Organizing it all would be a very important job. Do you think you can manage it, troll?" asked Mrs Singh.

"Madam," said the troll indignantly, "have no fear. The Litter Brigade in the street will be very well organized. I shall make a rota of who is to help me, everyone will have to help once every two weeks. Just you watch and see – this is going to be the tidiest and the greenest and most earth-friendly street in town."

That very day the troll pulled up the notices that warned trespassers of what would happen to them, and that night he didn't go out on his patrol. But early the next morning he rang Darren's doorbell.

"Come on, rise and shine. I need your help on the Litter Brigade. Come on now, half an hour before you go to school and half an hour when you come back."

Darren staggered out of bed, and after that every day someone was woken up to help

the troll sort the rubbish. The
street continued to look lovely
and soon the streets around
wanted the troll to come and
organize a Litter Brigade for
them. The troll became very
important and a much-loved
figure in the neighbourhood.

Often he was seen having ice-cream with someone or playing with a group of children.

After a while he got a bike so that he could cycle around supervising all the Litter Brigades and as he rode round the streets he could be heard singing:

"I'm a troll, fol-de-rol,
I'm a troll, fol-de-rol,
I'm a troll, fol-de-rol,
And I sort litter to earn my
supper."